EARN YOUR WINGS!

By Mary Tillworth

A Random House PICTUREBACK® Book

Random House New York

rhcbooks.com

ISBN 978-0-525-64580-1

Printed in the United States of America

10 9 8 7 6 5 4 3 2 1

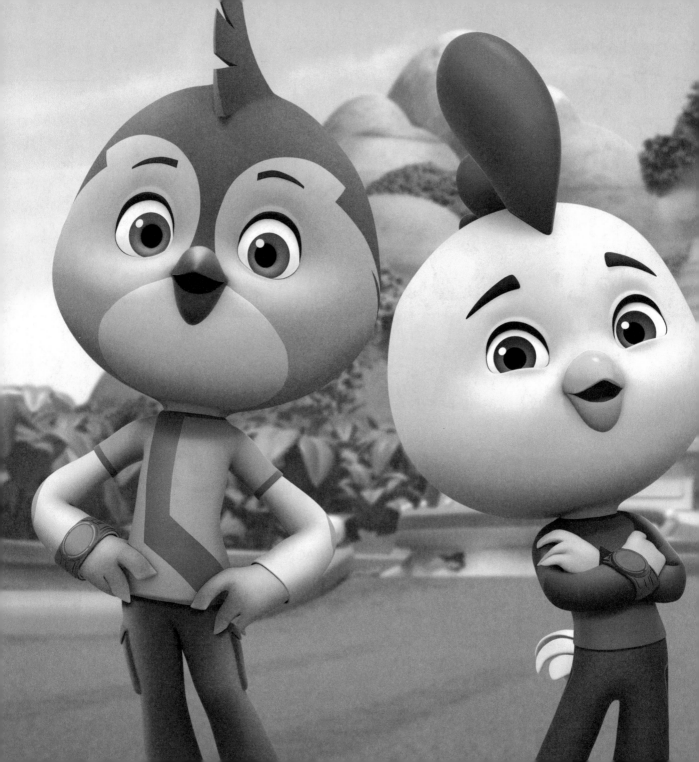

The high-flying cadets at Top Wing Academy are ready to earn their wings! Swift, Rod, Penny, and Brody flock together to learn new skills and become full-feathered rescue flyers on Big Swirl Island.

Team Top Wing flies into action!

SWIFT is the name, and speed is his game! As the leader of Team Top Wing, this experienced blue jay does whatever it takes to keep his fellow cadets on track.

Swift can fly under his own wing power, but when he needs extra speed, his turbo-charged Flash Wing makes him the fastest pilot on the island. And his jet is equipped with grabber talons for swooping rescues!

PENNY the penguin is an underwater-rescue expert. She is fearless and smart, and uses her navigation skills to locate and track critters in trouble with her Aqua Wing submarine.

After a hard day of work, Penny loves to chill in a bathtub full of ice cubes with a frozen treat!

ROD the rooster is funny and full of energy.
His all-terrain Road Wing can get him where he
needs to be faster than the shake of a tail feather.
Rod's favorite saying is "Let's cock-a-doodle-DO
this!" With his can-do attitude, he's a great addition
to the Top Wing team.

When it comes to making a plan, laid-back **BRODY** would rather wing it. This sweet, happy-go-lucky puffin loves to surf the waves but is always ready to cruise into action with his Splash Wing speedboat.

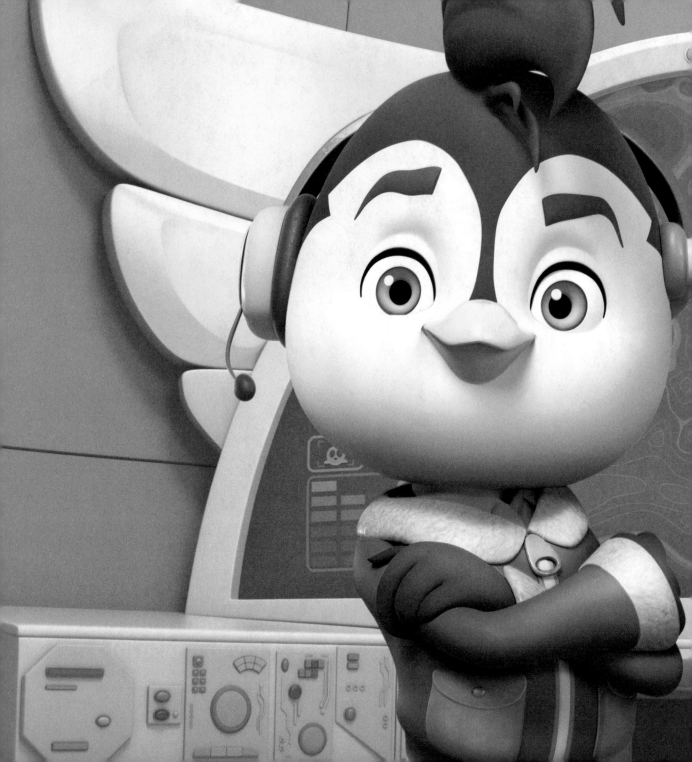

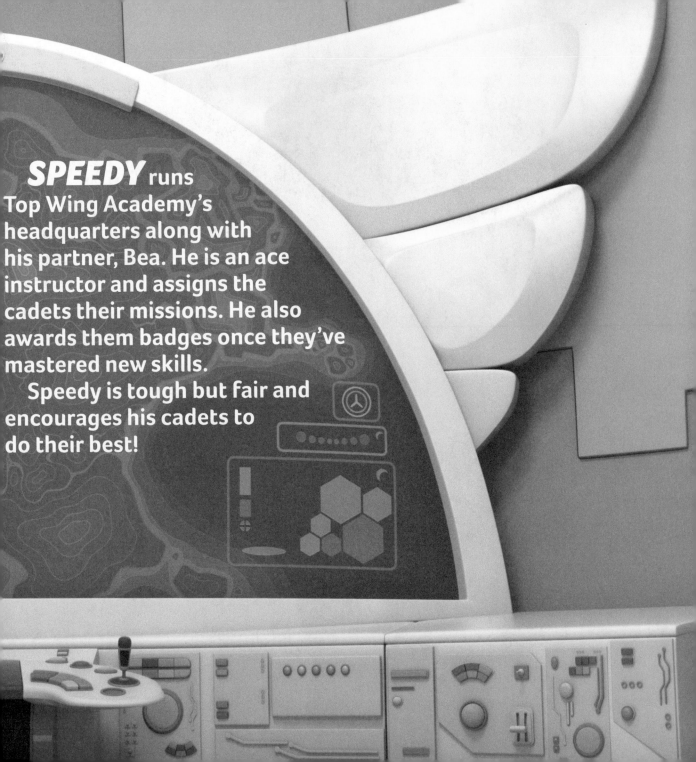

SPEEDY runs Top Wing Academy's headquarters along with his partner, Bea. He is an ace instructor and assigns the cadets their missions. He also awards them badges once they've mastered new skills.

Speedy is tough but fair and encourages his cadets to do their best!

BEA is a top-notch instructor and chief mechanic at the academy. Whether it's fixing an engine problem or adding a cool new gadget, she loves to get her wings dirty fixing the Top Wing vehicles.

CHIRP and **CHEEP** are chicks who like to poke their beaks into everything! They try to help Speedy and Bea, but their playful antics often get them in trouble. Luckily, the Top Wing team is there to pluck them out of danger!

SHIRLEY SQUIRRELY is a wide-eyed dreamer who wants
soar with the Top Wing team! But when she does something that
ets her in over her head, like accidentally turbo-charging her little
ane, Team Top Wing is there to fly her to safety.

RHONDA
the rhino is the friendly owner of the Lemon Shack. When the cadets need a refreshing drink or tasty snacks, they know exactly where to fly!

OSCAR the octopus plays music at the Lemon Shack. e can play a bunch of different instruments with his vesome tentacles!

No island is complete without a pair of swashbuckling pirates! **CAP'N DILLY** and **MATILD** are salty crocodiles who roam the sea surrounding Top Wing Academy, looking for treasure to take.

BADDY McBAT

thinks he's the baddest pilot
n Big Swirl Island. But when
e flies too close to danger,
he team takes wing to
ave him!

Penny, Swift, Brody, and Rod each have their own special skills. But they know that during every rescue, it's important to work together.

Under the watchful eyes of Speedy and Bea, the Top Wing team learns what it takes to make each mission a success.

GO, TEAM
TOP WING!